Mr S

Written and illustrated by
Jolyne Knox

Hamish Hamilton
London

For Julian Knox

HAMISH HAMILTON CHILDREN'S BOOKS

Published by the Penguin Group
27 Wrights Lane, London W8 5TZ, England
Viking Penguin Inc., 40 West 23rd Street, New York, New York 10010, U.S.A.
Penguin Books Australia Ltd, Ringwood, Victoria, Australia
Penguin Books Canada Ltd, 2801 John Street, Markham, Ontario, Canada L3R 1BR
Penguin Books (N.Z.) Ltd, 182–190 Wairau Road, Auckland 10, New Zealand

Penguin Books Ltd, Registered Offices, Harmondsworth, Middlesex, England

First published in Great Britain 1988 by
Hamish Hamilton Children's Books

British Library Cataloguing in Publication Data:
Knox, Jolyne
Mr. String.
I. Title
823'.914[J]   PZ7

ISBN 0–241–12260–0

Typeset by Kalligraphics Ltd, Redhill, Surrey
Printed in Great Britain by
Cambus Litho, Ltd
East Kilbride, Scotland

Mr Samuel String was a merry
musicmaker. Every day he played very
loud and very fast on his old violin. He
was a clever musician, but he was very
short-sighted and very forgetful. He was
always getting into dreadful muddles.

Mr String lodged in a ramshackle
old house. His proud landlady,
Mrs Miranda Muskett, tried hard to keep
'her Maestro' ship-shape.

6

One morning an important-looking
letter arrived. Mr String opened it
curiously.

"Oooh, my goodness me!" he cried.
"For the very first time I am invited to
play at the Royal Albert Hall. What a
thrill! My 'Rocket Concerto' will sound
good there."

He tied another knot in his
handkerchief and rushed to invite
Mrs Muskett to come too.

As the weeks before the concert went
by, Mr String lived in a hubbub of music.
Every day the house quaked as he
practised furiously to prepare for the big
night. Mrs Muskett tried in vain to keep
order.

At last the great day came. Mr String
awoke early and plunged into his bath.
He sang at the top of his voice as he
thought of the marvellous time he would
have playing at the Royal Albert Hall.
He would be like all the famous musicians
– with calls for ten encores perhaps. . .!

All day long the house was in turmoil.
Mrs Muskett busily cheered up the dusty
String concert suit with a stiff brush and a
hot iron. She made tasty sandwiches to
keep the Maestro's strength up.
Meanwhile, Mr String bounced wild notes
from the walls and lampshades as his bow
flew across the strings.

11

By the time the cuckoo on the wall
wheezed five o'clock, the practising,
pressing and polishing were done.
Mrs Muskett prepared an early supper
of buttered toast with a tasty kipper.
Afterwards, Mr String dozed dreamily
in front of the hot coals.

12

Then it was time to leave. He thanked
Mrs Muskett for all her help and said, "I
am most honoured, dear lady, that you
will be coming to share the fun."

He gave a little bow and hurried off to
catch his bus.

Mrs Muskett smiled proudly and went
to fix her best hat. She wanted to be
properly dressed for this important
occasion.

At the bus stop, Mr String beamed and bid everyone 'Good day.' There was a muffled mutter from the queue.

"Deary me, this won't do," he thought. "I'll give them a cheery tune or two."

Strangely they seemed glad when the bus came!

The conductor wagged his finger and said, "All weapons at the back of the bus, Maestro."

"Cheeky fellow," said Mr String to himself.

The bus crawled along. Mr String felt he would never get to the hall on time. But at last he arrived. He walked a short way, then suddenly – there it was – THE ROYAL ALBERT HALL!

16

Mr String gazed in awe. It seemed even more splendid than he had expected.

"Oh, gosh," he thought, "what an evening this will be."

Tingling nervously, he went to find the artists' entrance.

At the back of the building a few people were waiting to see the performers arrive.

"Odd-looking music lovers," thought Mr String, feeling uneasy.

The doorman said, "Evening sport, which one are you, The Grappling Gorilla or Musclecrush Lou?"

Mr String was startled but he went inside boldly.

Suddenly, a big man in a vest appeared.

"Want a rub down, matey?" he grinned.

Mr String jumped. "Thank you," he said, trying to look dignified, "that will not be necessary."

Shaking nervously, he went into the dressing room and unpacked his violin.

Then, before he knew what had
happened, he was whisked towards a door
marked 'Arena'. From behind the door
there came a loud roaring noise.

"Oh deary, deary me," worried
Mr String, now very alarmed.

21

In a moment he was through the door. The noise nearly blew him over. High in a roped ring stood the most ferocious man he had ever seen. The Grappling Gorilla flexed his muscles. "Come on up, Maestro," he roared.

Inside Mr String's head a small doubt was growing into a very big one. He had muddled something REALLY important this time. What day was his concert anyway?

Before he could blink, Mr String was
gripped by The Gorilla.

"Oh, deary me!" he gasped as he was
whirled around. He struck the strings in a
fury of sparks. The Gorilla winced. On
they spun, getting giddier and dizzier.
Notes flashed all around. The Gorilla
puffed and grunted.

Suddenly, after a specially shattering
scale, The Gorilla wilted. He clapped his
hands to his ears.

"Cor," he groaned, "this is deadly,
mate. Let me out of 'ere!"

Amidst the uproar, Mr String was
named the victor. Amazed, he grinned
bashfully with relief.

The crowd cheered wildly. Musclecrush Lou, who had arrived late, gaped with astonishment as Mr String was given the shining, silver cup. He was the hero of the night.

"Now then, give my Maestro some room!" ordered Mrs Muskett, bustling through. "My stars, Maestro," she said, dusting Mr String down, "a proper pickle you've got yourself into this time. Who'd ever 'ave thought your concerts was so boisterous! Come home now and we'll 'ave a party to celebrate."

"Most kind, dear lady," said Mr String, bowing. He was feeling quite silly and rather sorry for the huge wrestlers, who were very crestfallen.

What a party it was! Everyone came. They all had bubbly champagne and sang and danced merrily late into the night.

Mr String soon forgot his embarrassment and invited them all to his *real* concert the very next day.

At last, as the stars faded into morning, Mrs Muskett shooed them off home and Mr String to bed.

As he fell asleep, dreaming happily, the silver cup seemed to wink at him.

"Tomorrow," he thought, "I shall be famous for my sparkling solos; but tonight, I am Maestro, THE CHAMP!"

30